*The Shadow of the Coachman's Body*

ALSO BY PETER WEISS

*The Aesthetics of Resistance: A Novel*
*Conversation of the Three Wayfarers*
*Marat/Sade*

# The Shadow
# of the Coachman's Body

## Peter Weiss

*translated from the German
and with an afterword by Rosmarie Waldrop
and with illustrations by the author*

A NEW DIRECTIONS PAPERBOOK

Originally published as *Der Schatten des Körpers des Kutschers* by Suhrkamp
Verlag in 1960

First published as New Directions Paperbook 1527 in 2022
Manufactured in the United States of America

*Library of Congress Cataloging-in-Publication Data*
Names: Weiss, Peter, 1916–1982, author. | Waldrop, Rosmarie, translator.
Title: The shadow of the coachman's body / Peter Weiss ; translated
from the German and with an afterword by Rosmarie Waldrop.
Other titles: Schatten des Körpers des Kutschers. English
Description: New York : New Directions Publishing Corporation, 2022.
Identifiers: LCCN 2021057646 | ISBN 9780811231619 (paperback) |
ISBN 9780811231626 (ebook)
Subjects: LCGFT: Novels.
Classification: LCC PT2685.E5 S313 2022 | DDC 833/.914—dc23/eng/20211203
LC record available at https://lccn.loc.gov/2021057646

10  9  8  7  6  5  4  3  2  1

New Directions Books are published for James Laughlin
by New Directions Publishing Corporation
80 Eighth Avenue, New York 10011

*The Shadow of the Coachman's Body*

Through the half-open door I see the muddy, trampled path and the rotten planks around the pigsty. The snout of the pig sniffs along the wide crevice whenever it isn't rooting in the mud, snorting and grunting. Besides this I also see part of the house, its wall with the yellowish plaster cracked and partly crumbling off, a few posts with horizontal pegs for the clothes lines, and farther back, as far as the horizon, moist black soil. These are the sounds: the smacking and grunting of the pig's snout, the slopping and splattering of the mud, the bristly rubbing of the pig's back against the planks, the squeaking and cracking of the planks, the rattling of the planks and loose posts at the wall of the house, the occasional soft whistling of the wind at the corner of the house and the gusts of wind sweeping over the furrows, the croaking of a crow far away which hasn't been repeated yet (it cried harm), the soft creaking and crackling in the wood of the little house where I sit, the dripping of the last of the rain from the tar-paper roof, hollow and hard when a drop hits a stone or the ground, plinking when a drop hits a puddle, and the rasping of a saw, from the shed.

The jerky back-and-forth of the saw, now stopping for a moment, now violently starting up again, indicates that it is in the hand of the hired man. Even without this special characteristic, often heard and confirmed and verified, I would not find it hard to guess that the hired man is handling the saw. Aside from him, only I take care of the wood in the shed, and on rare occasions the captain but only early in the morning and with unmistakable slowness; unless of course a new boarder has just arrived and, wishing to recover from the stiffness in his bones after the long coach trip, might be using the saw, bending forward and drawing backward with a taut back and thrusting and pulling with his arm. But I haven't heard the coach come in, neither the clopping of the wheels and straps, nor the rumble of the body, neither the horn signal that the coachman usually gives on arriving nor the tongue clicking nor the drumming sound he makes with his tongue to tell the horse to stop. Nor have I heard the stamping of the horse, and on the wet dirt road I certainly would have been able to hear it. And if the boarder had arrived on foot it is unlikely that he would go straight to the shed, and even if he had stepped into the shed, maybe from curiosity, his tiredness after the long hike (a day's walk from the nearest town) and the thick and shapeless pieces of root and trunk would have kept him from work. I insist then that it is the hired man who, in the shed, thrusts the saw into the heavy logs and pulls it back and forth; I see him in front of me in his shirt that was once blue but has long faded and is crusty with dirt and his equally crusty, once black, pants which he has tucked into the legs of his clumsy boots, also black once but plastered with dung and mud. I see him in front of me holding the piece of wood on the jack with one earthy, thick-veined, short-fingered hand while spanning the handle of the saw with the other, pushing his long lower lip over his short upper lip and licking off the slime trickling from his nose; I hear him humming from his throat, cooing as he does when working in the house or outside; and in the short, irregular stops between the sawing I can imagine him straightening his back, and bending far backward and stretching his arms out on both sides and cracking his knuckles, or blowing his nose with his thumb and index finger and then wiping it with the back of his hand, or pushing his greasy cap with ear flaps turned up off of his forehead far back on his head and softly scratching his thin, sticky strands of hair creased by the sweat band of his cap. Only now (the crow is just crying harm again) I feel cold on my bare seat. Writing down my observations has kept me from pulling my pants up and buttoning them; or the sudden start of my observations made me forget to pull up my pants; or maybe it was the lowered pants, the shivering, the concentration coming over me here in the outhouse that brought about this particular mood for observation. I now pull up my pants, button them and buckle the belt; I take the wooden lid, but before putting it on the opening I look down into the bucket filled to the brim with the brownish mass of excrement and paper with brown stains; as far as I can tell in the darkness of the box, the feces have even overflowed the rim of the bucket; the thick stream ends in a lava-like mound in which the bucket is half buried; the brightness of the shreds of paper gleams out of the black. After putting the lid on I sit down again on the box, the writing pad on my knees. The inside walls of the outhouse are covered with grainy tar paper; however, the moisture has made the paper bulge with enormous boils, and in some places it is torn and hanging down in tatters; the thin, moldy gray slats are bare underneath. A few rusty nails stick out of the wall, perhaps meant to hang clothes on or some utensils, but now empty and bent; not even a piece of string, a wire or a bundle of paper is hanging there. As for paper, everyone rips as much as he needs from the torn-up newspapers stacked at the corner of the seat. Now and then, after much reminding, the hired man brings these newspapers from the basement where they lie in a heap beside the coal, crumpled and dusty, having been used as wrapping around some delivered merchandise or left by travelers and read again and again, greasy, worn out, often put to further use in the kitchen, full of black skillet rims and imprints of plates and cups, with potato peels and fish bones sticking to them. And here, in the outhouse, these remains of newspapers with most of their information many years old, find another reader; sitting bent forward, one's feet propped on the ledge in front of the box, one gets absorbed in small, mixed-up fragments of time, in events without beginning or end, often even divided crosswise or up and down; one follows one person's speech and continues with the speech of another, one reads the description of the scene of an action and then glides on to the scene of a different action, one learns something which is denied in the next piece and yet proven to exist again in the one following that; one finds similar events furnished again and again with new details, or even comes across the same, here fitted with certain archaisms and there with some innovation. I shove my left foot forward, prop my writing arm on my right leg and push the door a bit further open. I now see the entire back wall of the house rising high and bare over the pigsty, with pointed gable and a roof which comes out far beyond the side walls, and one of the side walls, foreshortened, with the stone steps to the kitchen door, the stairs to the basement, and the narrow recesses of the windows, one of which, the window of the family's room, is open; a few pieces of cloth, probably diapers, are spread out on the sill. The ground around the house is, like the road and the fields, muddy and full of puddles; here and there are stones, large and small, some loose rubble, some sticking out of the ground with a whitish curve or edge, some heaped into small pyramids, some arranged in rows according to form and size; next to one of the heaps, a crowbar and a shovel are sticking in the ground. On the smooth handles of these tools I can imagine Mr. Schnee's hands, unusually large, bony hands with fingernails arched like shields; his work accumulates dirt under their long edges which right after work, however, is carefully removed with a silver nail file which Mr. Schnee keeps in the pocket of his vest. The stones too have gone through Mr. Schnee's hands, they have been felt, turned, and rolled over in his fingers; we can assume that he is now standing at the window of his room and looking down at the yard, waiting for the sun to dry the heaps of stones. In the course of time, he has dug up and examined large quantities of stones; many stones which he considered unsuitable he has carted in a wheelbarrow to a heap behind the woodshed, other stones which he plans to study he has carried up to his room where he keeps them on shelves all around the walls.

I am now in my room since the outhouse had to be used by another boarder whom we call the tailor because he sews his own clothes from old rags. The tailor appeared on the kitchen steps and walked toward the outhouse, in slippers, tiptoeing cautiously around the puddles, his head lowered, a pipe in his mouth. I cleared my throat and he was startled. He was terribly upset, a state he always gets into when meeting one of the other boarders unexpectedly; the pipe dropped out of his mouth, and while he bent down and fumbled for it, his glasses, held together by a thin wire, slid from his nose. His hands were burrowing in the yellowy mud water; I helped him, handed him the glasses and the pipe, and for a while he tried to put the glasses as a pipe into his mouth and the pipe as glasses to his eyes until finally the things found their proper places; drops of wet mud ran down his face. He wanted to turn and go back, but he was stuck; his hands alternately flapping up and down and wrung together; he was still standing that way after I had left him and was walking along the path toward the kitchen steps. Looking up to the house I saw, as I had suspected, Mr. Schnee standing at his window; his big, pale face to the pane, like a fish with his flattened nose, his broad, pouting lips licking the glass, and the bulging, colorless eyes. Walking by the open window on the ground floor, I had a short look into the family's room. I noticed the father, the mother, the infant, and the son in the following distribution and relation to each other: the mother sitting on the edge of the bed at the back of the room, half in the dark, her breast bared, and the infant at her breast; the father standing at the table in the middle of the room, his fists propped on the tabletop in front of him, the light from the window full on him, outlining the face thrust forward with the mouth wide open; and opposite him, not sitting but squatting on his heels, the son, his chin pressed against the edge of the table, his shoulders pulled up to the ears, staring into the father's open mouth. Then I reached the stairs, and this is the way I went to my room: I opened the kitchen door and closed it behind me; I went across the worn

gray linoleum of the kitchen which was moist from being scrubbed, and where the housekeeper was on her
knees and elbows, the scouring cloth in her hand, looking up at me in silence as I passed, with her thin dress
wet at the loins and arms and tightly clinging to the
heavy curves of her body. My next goal was the threshold of the opening to the hall; this I approached while
the objects in the kitchen were gliding by: at my right,
the stove with the flue of white-painted brick above it,
a pot of potatoes, a second pot full of carrots bubbling
on the fire, next to the stove the sink at the wall, filled
with plates and cups, and the table, below the window,
dusted with flour, with rolled dough on a board and
a few big kneaded lumps of dough, a wooden rolling
pin, a bowl of sugar and a spoon, and at each long side
of the table a slim bench stained dark as well as a stool
at each of the narrow sides of the table; to my left the
huge cupboard, its doors and drawers shut, next to it
the grandfather clock of brown wood, under its glass
the pendulum ticking slowly back and forth in front
of the weights in the shape of fir cones. After having
reached the threshold I had my next goal in front of
me, the stairs rising narrow and steep from the hall;
there is some dim light from an overhead window;
its bluish shimmer, aided by the pale light from the
kitchen, barely lights the space. I grazed the edge of
the sewing machine which had faint silver reflections
on its spools and metal parts, went by the round table in
whose open drawer I more assumed than saw buttons,

hooks, needles and thread, and hit the silk lampshade above it with my shoulder; it swayed back and forth with softly fluttering tassels. Then I passed Schnee's armchair letting my hand glide over the wooden arm rest and the straight, high back with its round tacks in the leather; back to back with this armchair is the captain's armchair on three legs; instead of the fourth, a couple of bricks support it; both the seat and the back have split open and show the plaited cords and the springs; above the back which is decorated with a wooden knob (of the other missing knobs only the peg holes bear witness) there hung some straps and a belt with a scabbard. Next to the empty umbrella stand and the empty coat hooks I could make out the front door of the house in the half dark, but I took my eyes off it now that I had reached the stairs. I put my hands on the banisters and climbed step after step on the red-dish rug which is fastened down with brass rods; my hands pulled me and my feet under which the steps were creaking pushed me higher and higher; above, I saw the landing which turns into the hall of the second floor. I reached the landing with a last pull of my arms while my hands held on to the top knobs on the banis-ters. Before being able to climb the stairs up to the attic I had to traverse the length of the hall. On both sides of the hall there are, one beside the other, the doors to the rooms of the hired man, the housekeeper, the cap-tain, the doctor, Mr. Schnee and the tailor, brown doors with brass handles and keyholes; and up high, in the lightshaft over the stairs, one can see the bluish glass of the garret window. The narrow rug runs from the stairs through the hall; its black edges look like rails, and walking along I seemed to be rolling in a car to the attic stairs. Here, I again put my hands on the banisters and climbed to the last but one goal, the attic. Up there I saw my last goal in front of me, the door to my room; and I went toward this door under the rafters, past the high square beams that carry the weight of the roof, past the boxes, baskets and suitcases that are stored under the rafters, past the chimney until I could reach the door handle with my hand; but this moment is long past, the moment of opening the door, of entering, of receiving the image of the room, of closing the door, of the way to the table; past also is the time that has gone by with the description of my way here. I am now lying stretched out on my bed.

Besides the daily operations of dressing and undressing, washing, going to bed and getting up, and the attempts at writing which have never yet gone beyond always new, short, broken-off beginnings, my activity in this room is to bring up images. For this, I lie stretched out on the bed; within reach, beside me, on the table, there is a plate full of salt from which I occasionally take a few grains to put in my eyes. The function of the salt is to stimulate the tear glands and thus blur my vision; the resulting tear threads, light points, and swelling or dissolving wedges of light are superimposed on the image of the room which is clearly

etched into my retina; and even though this room contains nothing but a table, a chair, a washstand, a bed,
and even though there is nothing on the sloping wall
but the window above the table, and only a door in the
opposite, straight wall, and nothing on the two other
walls which are cut by the roof, even so my look is still
trapped by these limits and fixed forms; with my tears
I dissolve them. While I look straight ahead with wide-
open eyes, the uncertain, flickering shadows, beams,
prisms, splotches of color, and lines gradually gather
into the first suggestions of figures, interrupted, in the
beginning, by sudden tinges of total black. The results
of these experiments on which I've spent hardly more
than ten minutes, at most a quarter of an hour, are as
follows: first, I discerned a curve, like a balloon or a
glass ball of indefinite color, sometimes tending toward
green, sometimes toward yellow or blue, and growing
more and more luminous and intense. This ball could
be a lamp or simply some big decoration hanging down
into a room; around the ball, colored ribbons of shiny
silk or thin metal joined, and the ball grew upward with
new curves, swellings, grooves like those that grow out
of clay on the wheel, in the hands of the potter. The
shape radiated in the colors of the rainbow against a
black background from which new details now came
forward. Dappled planes in purple and pink suggested
depth; however, one could not see the space as a whole;
it seemed to dissolve into the infinite. From the background, which was constantly shifting and sometimes
showed a moving marbled wall or a piece of a polished

floor, emerged single smaller balls, these too shimmering in a glassy fire, and figures like castles from a game of chess or ballet dancers; they were of the same material as the balls, but their shape more ephemeral; while the balls were stretching and expanding, the figures changed without pause, they resembled plants, minerals, sculptures, crystals, or simply rose as undefinable beings from the dark, a mere play of colors and shapes. Holding my breath I followed their movements until suddenly, after I had felt the picture fading and put a few more grains of salt in my eyes, the scene changed. Now it was as though I were leaning against the railing of a balcony, high over a city at night; the indefinable space of the former image gave way to the distinct hugeness of a celestial dome. Deep down there was a street with roofs spread out around it, but the street was no more than a black ravine, or just a narrow crack; and directly below me, on the roof garden of the house opposite, there gleamed a face as if in moonlight, yet there was no moon nor any stars, a face with thin cheekbones, a full, dark mouth, dark shaded eyes, and under the face a slim throat against the flowing hair, and under the edge of the throat the sharply outlined collar bone with the bare straight shoulders, and under the shoulders the bare breasts circumscribed by lines of shadows, with the black centers of the nipples, and under the breasts the ribs suggested by dim shadows and the smooth bare round of the belly with the dark center of the navel, and under the belly the triangular dark of the womb and the slim angular hips, and

under the hips, down to the cut-off line of the stone parapet, the long curves of the thighs; I bent over the railing toward the female body; I felt her nearness so strongly that I took the mirage for reality and made a hasty movement with my arms which immediately tore the image.

We eat supper, like all other meals, at the kitchen table. In spite of the wealth of dishes in the cupboard, the table is set with a minimum of plates, cups, bowls, and silverware, so that a possible appetizer and a possible dessert are eaten on the same plate as the main course, a deep plate of white china. For eating tools, each uses only one tin spoon for all the courses as well as for stirring in the mug from which he drinks his water, beer, wine or coffee. Not much store is set on the cleanliness of the tabletop, in contrast to the floor which is scrubbed several times daily by the housekeeper; thus the table is still full of flour and lumps of dough, and of dried breadcrumbs and gristle from former meals. This is the order in which the boarders are sitting around the table: on the stool at the upper narrow side of the table, next to the stove, the housekeeper; to her left, on the bench in front of the wall with the window, the captain in a black old-fashioned cutaway with white stripes, like pants, a gray vest which, in spite of his painstaking care, has not escaped a few spots in the course of the years, a white shirt with a high stand-up collar, and a black tie fastened with a pearl clasp; to the left of the captain, Mr. Schnee, who in the evening is wrapped in his silk house coat; to the left of Mr. Schnee, the doctor with thickly bandaged head, a band-aid across his nose and a band-aid on his upper lip, a bandage around his neck, bandages around his wrists, enormously thick bandages on his legs, his mouth shut tight over the pain that seems to fill his whole body and threatens to break from his mouth, his eyes hidden behind black glasses. At the other narrow side of the table, the hired man is sitting with his cap on his head; to his left, at the other long side of the table, the tailor in his threadbare pieced-together suit, piebald as a harlequin, describing, since he has prepared himself for this meeting, large curves, capricious arabesques, and wild angles with gestures so calculated that they constantly outgrow themselves. To the left of the tailor, I am sitting. To my left, nobody; the place is empty and waiting for a new boarder. (The family who live in the room next to the kitchen do not take part in our meals; they keep house for themselves.) In the middle of the table are the two pots, one filled with potatoes, the other with carrots. Hands holding spoons are now lifted toward the pots from all sides; the housekeeper's hand red, swollen, dishwaterlogged; the captain's hand with polished, grooved fingernails; the doctor's hand with bandage slings between all fingers; the hired man's hand spotty with dung and mud; the tailor's hand trembling, skinny, like parchment; my own hand, my own hand; and then no hand, in an empty space waiting for a hand. The spoons dip into the pots and come out laden with potatoes and carrots, discharge their load onto the plates and swing back to the pots, fill up, unload over the plates, continue to wander back and forth until each has assembled on his plate a heap of potatoes and carrots according to his appetite. The biggest heap is on the hired man's plate, but the heap on the tailor's plate is nearly as big although the tailor doesn't, like the hired man, spend most of his day outside in strenuous physical labor, but only sits in his room over his rags; next, the heap on the housekeeper's plate, barely distinguishable (and only after several precise comparisons) from the heap on Schnee's plate; then the captain's heap which is already small compared with the heap on the hired man's plate; then the heap on my own plate which can be called little, but still seems big in relation to the heap on the doctor's plate. Now the spoons full of pieces of potatoes and carrots rise to the mouths; the mouths open: the housekeeper's mouth as if for a sucking kiss while she wheezingly blows through her nose; the captain's mouth cautiously maneuvering his false teeth; Schnee's mouth with the broad lips pulled back, bared and whitish; the doctor's mouth splitting in a painful crevice; the hired man's mouth pushed forward like a beak, the tongue sticking way out expecting the spoon; the tailor's mouth popping open foppishly and widening to lockjaw; my own mouth, my own mouth; and then the empty space for a new, still unknown mouth. Thus we chew our first bite: the housekeeper slowly, circular, grinding; the captain gnashing his false teeth; Schnee smacking his lips and bending over his plate; the doctor gulping without moving his teeth, mashing his food with his tongue against his palate; the hired man slurping, his arms heavy on the table; the tailor leering at the hired man's plate, his jaw muscles trembling and sticking out like cords, his tongue licking the spittle-soaked pap; I, I; and then the one whose chewing I don't know about. This is the way we eat, silently; the hired man, the tailor, and the housekeeper load their plates another time; they, however, catch up with the other eaters so that we all finish about the same time. Between movements of the spoons, the tin mugs are occasionally grabbed by the other hands; the housekeeper's mug is filled with beer; the captain's mug is filled with water; Schnee's mug is filled with dark red wine which he poured from a bottle kept in the pocket of his house coat; the doctor's mug contains a few drops of water; the hired man's mug is filled with beer; the tailor's mug is filled with water, as is my own, and what would the unknown boarder fill his mug with. The mugs are lifted to the mouths and the liquid penetrates into the mouths, fills the mouths except with the doctor who only moistens the split in his mouth, thin as a notch from a knife. While the hand's grip on the spoon is nearly the same with all, each distinguished rather by his way of raising his hand: with the housekeeper, arm and hand keep a nearly fixed position and it is the upper part of her body that goes up and down; the captain makes a cracking lever movement with his elbow;

Schnee's hand moves the spoon from the wrist back and forth between the plate and his lowered mouth; the hired man's hand pushes the spoon like a coal shovel into his mouth gaping like a furnace door in front of the plate; the tailor's arm jerks and jumps like a wound-up doll; I, I hardly notice how I eat for watching the others—the grip on the mug is strongly characteristic with each: the housekeeper takes the mug with a rounded hand, she slides her hand under the mug and lifts it in her hand as in a bowl toward the mouth; the captain puts the tips of his crooked fingers on the mug, holds the mug as in the tongs of a bird's claw; Schnee feels the mug with his long bone-white fingers, and while he lifts the mug his fingers seem to milk it; the doctor presses the mug between his free hand and the hand that holds the spoon, and, in a concerted effort, both hands clamp the mug to the mouth; the hired man puts his hand around the mug like a mound of earth and tips the mug into the approaching mouth; the tailor who, when not drinking, keeps his flat hand as a lid on the mug, flips his hand sideways for drinking, then snaps his thumb down and his fingers around and moves the mug as in a box; I myself feel the cool roundness of tin in the inside of my hand. The following incidents happened during the meal: at the beginning, when we had hardly taken our seats, one could hear the cawing of the crow from the fields; it was a single cry sounding like harm as before. When our spoons began scraping the full plates we heard through the wall also the clatter of dishes on the family's table; the infant blubbered, but calmed down soon, probably being given suck; a sound like a tin spoon hitting a tin mug and then a few seconds complete silence behind the wall were followed by another noise, like a belt coming down hard on a body, repeated several times until there was silence again; soon after, the usual clanking of dishes continued. A coughing fit of the tailor's was, beside the doctor's one smothered groan, the only interruption of the monotony of our meal; the only other thing to be noted is the appearing and disappearing of a black medium-sized bug; it fell from the flue onto the top of the stove, was lucky enough to land on its legs (if it had fallen on its back the heat of the stove would have charred it) and quickly ran to the edge of the stove from where it looked down into the sink. Its forelegs felt for the start of the sink, the body followed, and that way he slid down; I stood up and saw it disappear into one of the holes of the strainer. Which death, I asked myself, is easier for a beetle, or less painful, death by burning on a stove or death by drowning in a drainpipe. We drink our coffee in the hall after the plates, stacked by the boarders, have been carried to the sink by the housekeeper, and the mugs, filled from the blue pot by the housekeeper, have been carried through the kitchen by the boarders, and the boarders have taken a piece of sugar from the sugarbowl the housekeeper has brought from the larder, put it in the cup, and have crossed the threshold and sat down in the hall stirring in their mugs with spoons which all but the doctor have licked clean: the housekeeper on the chair in front of the sewing machine, the captain on his armchair supported by bricks, back to back with the armchair where Mr. Schnee has sat down, the doctor on the umbrella stand, the hired man on a folding chair he had pulled from under the stairs, the tailor completely in the shadow on the floor near the front door, and myself on the third step of the stairs. Hardly has everyone found his place and put the edge of the mug to his lips and felt the black, hot coffee run to the tip of his tongue, when the door to the family's room opens and the father comes out, also holding a tin mug, which he is stirring with a tin spoon, and after him the mother, with the same kind of mug and spoon, and after the mother the son, carrying a chair in each hand. He puts the chairs down between the housekeeper's chair and the armchairs of the captain and Mr. Schnee and pushes them under the father and mother who sit down on the chairs; then he turns and goes back into the room and shuts the door behind him. The monotony of the common meal in the kitchen grows here, in the hall, into a diversity of occurrences. The mere irregular distribution of boarders in the room makes right away for a pattern of interconnected movements and sounds that is hard to survey. The housekeeper puts her mug on the sewing machine and reaches into the drawer of the sewing table where the buttons rattle in her fingers; the tailor scrapingly pulls

up his legs and crosses them, then he takes his pipe
from his hip pocket and begins stuffing it with tobacco
which he has pulled out of his side pocket; the captain
too reaches into a pocket, his vest pocket, takes out a
silver case, knocks on the lid, snaps the lid open, leans
over the back of the armchair, hands the case over
Schnee's shoulder; Schnee turns toward him, thrusts
his hand with a wide curve into the case, lifts a cigarette out of it whereupon the captain takes the case
back, takes a cigarette out of the case himself, snaps the
case shut and puts it back into his vest pocket. Then
the captain reaches into his pants pocket and makes his
hand come out with a lighter; the hand with the lighter
swings over the back of the armchair, Schnee turns his
face toward the lighter, the captain's fingers strike fire,
and Schnee sucks at the flame with the cigarette in his
mouth. The face of the captain turned over the back is
close to Schnee's face, the eyes of both of them look
sideways at the lighter, and the flame is reflected in
their pupils; after the tip of Schnee's cigarette starts
glowing and he blows a cloud of blue smoke from his
lips, the captain puts the flame to his own cigarette,
and Schnee watches him sucking on the cigarette, and
this cigarette too starting to glow, and the smoke flowing from the captain's mouth. The father leans forward
and takes the scabbard which has been hanging on the
back of the armchair since the afternoon when the captain probably busied himself with it; he lifts it up to
himself and fingers it; the captain turns to him, takes

hold of the belt fastened to the scabbard, pushes the scabbard farther toward the father, but without letting go of the belt. While they are exchanging words which I cannot hear because of the distance and their talking softly, the captain leans still more toward the father, the belt in his hand, the father runs his finger along the scabbard up to the belt and puts his index finger into the sheath. Schnee too turns toward the scabbard and of the words which he contributes to the conversation I distinguish: rust and clean. Meanwhile the mother has moved closer to the housekeeper, and between her and the housekeeper there are also words exchanged of which I understand a few, like pap, threading, airing, the boy, take care of the baby, wash dishes later, for Sunday, give food, give suck, hurt, pinches so. The housekeeper has pulled a linen shirt from the lower drawer of the table and starts sewing a button where the collar begins; Schnee takes a few small stones from one pocket of his house coat (the neck of the bottle is sticking out of the other), weighs them in his hand and holds them over the scabbard, under the eyes of the captain and the father; the lines of vision gather with Schnee's own into a bundle on the stones; I hear some of the words from the series of statements that Schnee pronounces: for instance, especially, dried out, streaked, just two more, will try tomorrow, sometime deeper, from that point, still not, after all, if one some-time, might be. The father reaches with the hand he had put into the sheath for the stones and fingers them, and among his words I discern: have of course, maybe

work, just hangs around, good for nothing, will ask him right away. At that he turns toward the door to the family's room and whistles between his teeth; from the room we can hear a crash as if a chair were falling over, the door is thrown open, and the son appears, runs over the threshold with hunched shoulders, leaves the door open behind him, runs through the hall past the chairs of the mother and the housekeeper, runs, bumping into the lamp which sways back and forth with fluttering tassels, to the father's chair. The father lifts his hand and hooks his index finger into the uppermost buttonhole of the son's jacket while keeping hold of his mug with his thumb, middle finger, ring finger and little finger, and pulls the son's torso down to his ear. In the family's room which is lit by a bulb hanging from the ceiling, I can see the infant lying on the green cover of the bed, his legs in the air, groping with his hands for his feet, sometimes getting hold of a toe and losing it again, straining to raise his head and letting it fall back again. From the conversation into which the son is drawn I get the following: words of the father's like early, usefulness, Mr. Schnee's activity, looked on long enough, show for once, barrow, shovel, sand, seven, eight, nine stones, cart away, clean, line up; words said by Mr. Schnee like of course, be cautious, careful, understand what about, three thousand seven hundred seventy-two stones to date, learn from the beginning, count on remuneration too; interjected words of the captain's like better, very well, not the worst, in my time, much changed. During the negotiations, the son is not looking at the father and not at Mr. Schnee or the stones in front of him, but across at me; his hair hangs into his knitted brows, his lips rub against his teeth, and his skin twitches around his deepset, black eyes staring out of the white. The mother whose face had been lowered over the housekeeper's work, straightens up now and leans over sideways with her hand stretched out to the son; she pulls at the hem of his jacket; Schnee snaps the long nail of his index finger against one of the stones; the captain pulls the scabbard back to himself; it slides slowly through the father's hand; the mother tugs at the hem of the son's jacket; the jacket is raised by the son's shoulders; through the mother's pulling the jacket slides down along with the sinking shoulders of the son, until the hem of the jacket is hanging over his knees like a skirt and his shoulders have subsided to a tilted plane. The captain has pulled the scabbard from the father's hand, he raises the scabbard and lightly touches the son's hanging shoulder with it while the mother is still holding on to the hem of the son's jacket and the father's index finger is still hooked in the buttonhole of the jacket. From the dark under the stairs there are sounds that indicate a change in the situation, and I see now that the tailor has, probably on all fours, come up to the hired man, and probably because the hired man waved to him with a pack of cards. The hired man's hand deals the cards with flapping smacks on the floor so that a heap grows in front of him and another in front of the tailor. Then they arrange the cards in their hands, whereupon the hired man, bending far down from his folding chair, pulls out a card and throws it heavily on the floor, and the tailor, sitting with his legs crossed, makes the same gesture, only more elaborately. In this manner things go back and forth between them; and behind them, leaning his back against the umbrella stand, I can see the doctor, his face distorted with pain, one hand unwrapping the bandage from the wrist of the other. Between card throws, the hired man and the tailor now and then take a sip from the mugs they have put on the floor beside them; the captain and Mr. Schnee too occasionally take a sip from the mugs which Schnee is balancing on one of his knees and the captain has clamped between his two knees. The father also takes a sip from the mug pulling the son's chest down with his hooked finger, and also the mother, who has turned away from the son again, drinks from the mug she has placed on the sewing machine beside the housekeeper's mug; and also the housekeeper now and then interrupts her work and slurps a mouthful; and I also take a gulp from the mug whose warm roundness lies between my hands. The loose parts of the bandage at the doctor's wrist have blood and pus stains; he continues to unwrap while rolling up the loose part; and the housekeeper's hand with needle and thread glides up and down; and the mother tilts her head back and yawns with wide-open mouth; and the father's index finger lets go of the buttonhole in the son's jacket; and Schnee's hand with

the stones sinks back into the pocket of the house coat;
and the captain lifts the tails of his cutaway and buckles
the belt with the scabbard; and the doctor, with con-
torted mouth, tears the last bit of bandage from his
wrist and looks at the flaming red skin laid bare; and
the captain and Mr. Schnee lean their heads back so
that the backs of their heads touch; and the tailor,
the first round of the game done, is now shuffling the
cards; and the son tiptoes off backward toward the
open door to the family's room; and the housekeeper's
teeth bite off the thread; and the mother scratches under her breasts; and the doctor leaves his place and
comes toward the stairs holding the inflamed wrist in
his other hand; and the tailor deals the cards; and the
housekeeper rummages among the buttons in the
drawer and pulls out a new button which she holds
against the front of the shirt; and the son reaches,
walking backward, the threshold, steps over the
threshold, and pulls the door shut in front of him, going backward into the room; and the doctor walks past
me up the creaking steps; I move to the side; I hear him
groaning softly; in the baggy pocket of his jacket his
mug of coffee sploshing.

After everybody had retired to his room, except for the
housekeeper who went to the kitchen to wash the floor,
and after even the housekeeper, the job finished, had
turned out the light in the kitchen, the hall, and the
stairwell, and shut the door of her room behind her, I
heard again, lying on my bed, the noise, the shuffling,

hitting and screaming downstairs. Since this noise was familiar from other evenings I knew that it came from the family's room, and although the course of the disturbance was known I asked myself again, as always, whether I should go down to help, or interfere, or just stand in front of the door and wait. And as always, I remained lying down for a while thinking that the noise would stop by itself although I knew it would not stop by itself; I put a few grains of salt in my eyes, but no pictures came; I only heard the noise rise up the stairs in muted waves. Then I got up, I had already taken off my shoes, and went in stocking feet down the dark stairs. I stopped in front of the door of the family's room, and from behind the door I heard the cracking voice of the father, the blubbering of the infant, the sobbing of the mother, the panting breath of the son. My eyes gradually got used to the dark; high above the stairs I noticed the pale purple-blue square of the garret window; and the black of the hall was not so dark that I couldn't see the furniture as still darker shades of black. I bent down to the keyhole and peered into the room where the mother was sitting on the edge of the bed pressing the infant to her, and the father was running after the son around a chair which the son was holding in front of himself; the father had grabbed the hem of the son's jacket; the jacket was stretched taut, and the chest of the son pulling forward; and the father screamed words of which I got the following: will you, across my knee, what I, if you won't, will you, I tell you, that you, I'll; between these words there was a bubbling of words in which his tongue got tangled. Sobbing and rocking the infant in front of her breasts, the mother screamed words at the son each time he ran past her; and of her words which were partly drowned in the sobs and partly interrupted by the humming sounds with which she tried to calm the infant, I caught these: that you, how can you, it'll get, now lie down, deserved, otherwise you'll, now stop, you have to, now stand still, you'll make him, he'll get, he has to. All of a sudden, the son stopped so abruptly that the father bumped into him, nearly knocked him over, nearly lost balance himself, and they faced each other, staggering; but this lasted only a second; then the father, panting and already screaming again, slumped down on the chair he had pulled close and dragged the son, who didn't resist any more, down till he lay prone across his knee, whereupon the father, pulling at the seat of the son's pants, let his hand smack down on the flat, slim buttocks of the son stretched taut under the shiny material of the pants, again and again, while his voice uttered completely unrecognizable words among yodeling cries. The son lay still, his hands hanging down to the floor; and the mother, accompanying each of the father's blows with a jerky movement of her back, was urging the son, and among her unclear, weeping words I distinguished these: now I ask, now you have to, now ask, otherwise you'll, he's already. With each word she moved a bit farther forward on the edge of the bed until only the final edge of her bottom was leaning against the final edge of the bed. The son now started whining in high, artificial gutturals, and although his mouth was pressed against the hollow of the father's knee I heard the words he cried in his strained, distorted voice: I won't do it again, I won't do it again, I'll never do it again, never, never do it again. The father was still hitting the son with weakening strokes and screamed words of which I got the following: well now, now at last, now you see, so at last, but before, never again, will you ever, can you, how shall I, how can I, will you really, have I now. His words, like his blows, became feebler and feebler till both words and blows died down and nothing but a rattling groan came from his mouth. The son turned his face and looked up at the father's face which had taken on a chalky hue with blue spots on temples and cheeks. The father pressed his left hand against his chest, at the heart, with his right he was fumbling at his collar-button; his eyes were closed, his mouth open with exhaustion. Groaning, he rubbed his chest; and the son slowly glided down from the father's knees, the eyes of his rigid, expressionless face fixed on the father's face. The mother had put the infant, who began yelling shrilly, down on the cover of the bed and ran with her arms spread wide to the father. The father stiffly kicked his legs forward and reared up over the back of the chair; the mother took his arms, tilted her face up and shouted words at the ceiling of which I caught these: you see, brought on, have done, O that you, you with your, can't stand. The son stood bending slightly forward with hanging shoulders and hands dangling at his knees; his eye had turned away from the

father and fixed on the keyhole in the door as if he could see my eye in the darkness behind the keyhole. The mother, grabbing the father's head, kept on screaming while the father lay stiffly stretched across the chair, the heels of his boots propped on the floor, his back against the edge of the seat, the neck pressed against the back of the chair; and these are the words that were understandable among her stammering and screaming: O what's wrong, what's the matter, he done to you, O help help, not just look on, help help. She tried to turn the father's head and, when this failed, to loosen the father's hands, one of which was pressed against his heart, the other against his throat; and when this failed too, and the father kept lying across the chair, stiffly, with rattling breath, she hurried a few steps toward the door, turned around, tried the father's head and hands again, ran to the door again, and again back, shouting words of which I got these: O help help somebody, is nobody, anybody, don't let, help help, you've done, you've done, O help help. At these calls I opened the door and ran to the chair and put my hands under the father's shoulders and pulled him up, the mother helping by pushing from the back; we raised the stiff body up, but hardly was he upright when his knees, belly and neck bent, his hands fell down from the heart and throat, his arms dangled at the joints; the mother shouted: him to bed, quick bed; and so we dragged him between us to the bed; on the way to the bed, the mother pushed the son aside with an outward movement of her leg and shouted: you stand there, you look on, but help, is all. In front of the bed, she put the father in my arms with the words: hold him, just child aside; and I held the father, whose stale rattling breath wafted in my face, tightly until the mother had pushed the still bawling infant up on the pillow and turned to me again in order to lift the father's body onto the bed with me. While I let down his shoulders she pulled his legs from the floor and thus we put him on the bed lowering the upper part of his body and lifting the lower. Will end up killing him, the mother said to the son when the father was stretched out on the green cover, the red infant at his head, no longer crying but babbling curiously, diverted by the father's head beside him. The father opened his eyes and painfully turned his head sideways. The son sneaked over to the bed with hunched shoulders and, kneeling down in front of the bed, said as in a monotonous prayer: never again, never again, never do it again, never never do it again; and the father lifted his hand and felt for the son's neck, ear, and part of the hair, and from there the hand slid down over the temple, the cheek, and the chin of the son, while he groaned deeply. The mother who was standing with folded hands at the head of the bed nodded at me and wiped her eyes; and I slowly went backward to the door; the beaten son was kneeling in front of the father's bed murmuring his prayer; and the father's breath was getting more regular, and his skin gradually returned from the chalky pallor to its natural coloring. With my hand stretched out behind me, I reached the door handle, pressed it down, opened the door, went out backward and shut the door in front of me.

Since I am, for the first time, getting my notes beyond a beginning that ends in nothing, I continue keeping to the sensations that crowd in on me here in my immediate surroundings; my hand guides the pencil over the paper, from word to word and from line to line, although I clearly feel the counterforce in me which used to get me to break off my attempts and which even now whispers with each row of words that I form according to what I have heard and seen, that what I've heard and seen is too insignificant to be preserved and that I'm wasting in this manner my hours, half my night, perhaps even all my day to no purpose; but I counter this with the question: what else shall I do; and from this question grows the insight that my other activities also remain without result or purpose. Tracing the occurrences in front of my eyes with my pencil in order to give an outline to what I've seen, to make what I've seen clearer, in short, to make seeing into an occupation, I sit next to the shed, on the stack of wood whose knotty pieces of root plastered with earth, moss and withered leaves give out a bitter rotten smell. From my high seat I survey the rutted, muddy plane of the yard still not dry from the last downpours, bordered by the long side of the house with the steps to the kitchen and the steps to the basement. Back of the house, the dirt road can be seen; it gets lost between the fields, but one can trace its course by the telephone poles, and these poles go, getting smaller and smaller and moving closer and closer to each other, as far as the misty curve of the horizon. Looking to my right, I see the pigsty, above its rim the pig's ears limply flapping back and forth, and the pig's tail curling up; next, the outhouse, brownish black, with slashed tar paper on the slanted roof; and a few hens are moving around the outhouse, picking in the earth and the meager islands of grass; between their picking and scratching, they make clucking sounds. Looking to the left, I notice the heap of stones behind the shed, and behind the stone heap, the grange rises up surrounded by wheel tracks; and behind the grange, the fields are spread out; a horse is stamping along the furrows; and behind the horse, a plow is staggering, and behind the plow, half supported on the handle of the plow, the hired man is clomping; and back of the fields, there are woods in the reddish purple haze, and low above the woods there is the red sun breaking from steaming clouds, its light throwing a long black purple shadow wherever it hits a shape rising from the ground. The window to the family's room is open; the father is leaning on the sill; he is stretching his arms and his chest; and behind him the son can be seen, his elbows on the table. The father's movements are strong and full of expectation while the attitude of the son expresses feebleness and resignation; the slight movements of the mother's knees which, because of the limiting window frame, are the only visible parts of her body make me think that she is sitting on the edge of the bed and rocking the infant in her arms. The kitchen door opens and Schnee comes out, closes the door behind him and descends the steps of the kitchen stairs. The father turns to the son, takes hold of the son's wrist by swinging his arm backward, and pulls the son to his side at the window. Between the father and Mr. Schnee, the morning greeting takes place; I cannot grasp the wording, but I recognize it from the gestures: both nod their heads several times, the father stretches his hand out of the window, and Mr. Schnee reaches up to the window and takes the father's hand; they shake hands; then the father's head turns back and forth between Schnee and the son, and also his hand goes back and forth between the son and Schnee, from which I conclude that the father is repeating his offer of yesterday and wants to see it in effect. And sure enough he pushes the son up to the windowsill right after, Schnee raises his arms toward the son, and the son jumps down to him. Schnee and the son go side by side to the stones next to the house; Schnee's arm is resting on the son's shoulders.

The son, having under Schnee's direction gathered small and large stones from various places and filled the wheelbarrow with them (which actually neither helped Schnee nor saved him time since he bent down for every stone together with the son, having first pointed it out with his finger, then felt the stone with his fingers after the son had picked it up, and turned to watch the stone while the son put it on the heap, and bent over it again once it was on the heap, and with both hands took hold of the shovel which the son thrust into the heap of stones, and then lifted the shovel together with the son, or rather, lifted the shovel himself, its weight increased by the son's arms, and emptied the shovel into the wheelbarrow, dragging the son's hands and arms along on the shovel), came toward me with the wheelbarrow. Schnee had delegated this transfer of the stones to him; Schnee only followed him with his eyes, rounding his hands as if he himself were holding the handles and straining forward as if he himself were pushing the barrow. The son pushed the barrow toward me, bent over the handles with all his strength; he not only had to push the weight of the barrow forward through the mud, but also to balance the weight, always ready to sink to the left or right, in the middle over the wheel. He pushed the barrow toward me; and thick lumps of mud gathered on the wheel whose spokes half disappeared in the mud; mud also gathered on the son's shoes, white rubbers full of holes, and mud splattered his pants up to the knees. In order to get to the stone heap behind the shed, however, the son had to curve to the left with the barrow or, from the son's point of view, to the right; but he came straight toward me steering the barrow with difficulty; even when I pointed my hand to the left to draw his attention to the direction he had to take, he continued his way toward me; I waved my hand more violently and kept my arm stretched out to the left, but the wheel kept turning through the mud right at me. Schnee, back at the house, stretched out his right arm and pointed to the right; thus we both pointed in the same direction, Schnee by pointing to the right, and I by pointing to the left, the direction the son had to take in order to get to the stone heap; but the son pushed the barrow up to the wood stack; in front of the wood stack, right under my feet, he set it down. The son straightened up and looked at me; I was still holding my arm stretched to the left. The son turned to Schnee who was still holding his right arm stretched out; and in this moment, while the son turned to Schnee and back to the barrow and put his hands back on the handles and tensed his muscles to lift the barrow, I surveyed once more, still more exactly than before, the buildings and constituent parts of the landscape around me; I saw the tiles on the roof of the house shining in a moist, deep red, the weathervane on the chimney, and the thin bluish smoke rising from the chimney, and I saw the crystalline gleaming of grains of sand on the ground, and, on the horizon, a second cloud of smoke perhaps from a hunter's campfire or from a burning shed, and a rabbit hopping through the furrows, and the grass and thistles growing rankly on the fallow fields. Now the son had lifted the barrow and wanted to turn it to one side; the wheel had sunk into the mud up to the hub; he pulled and pushed, and, back at the house, Schnee pulled and pushed the air in front of him with rounded hands (his right arm had come down); but the barrow moved neither back nor forward, it only tilted to the right and to the left until, after a violent tug, it tipped over and with a rumble discharged its load. The son stood still for a while and looked down at the stones. The father leaned out of the window of the family's room and shouted words of which I got: do a job and show you; he gesticulated wildly with raised fist; and the son knelt down and began to put the stones one by one back into the barrow. I climbed down from the stack of wood and knelt beside the son in the soft mud and helped him fill the barrow with stones; and when the barrow was full I grasped the handles together with the son and pushed the barrow, in a concerted effort with the son, past the stack of wood toward the shed, and then past the shed to the stone heap. At the stone heap, we raised the handles and threw the stones from the barrow on the heap; and then the son turned the empty barrow and, by himself, pushed it along the rut back to Schnee who was waiting for him with dangling arms and who, after the son had joined him, continued his activities of bending down, picking up, gathering and loading. The father, leaning far out of the window with his arms folded on the sill, watched these activities. He watched the son bending over the stones together with Schnee and putting the stones in a heap and then thrusting the shovel into the heap and emptying the shovel into the barrow; and I also, back on the stack of wood, watched these activities when I noticed that, for some moments, even the housekeeper, who, upstairs in the house, had opened the window of her room in order to shake out her sheets, was watching these activities after having shaken the sheets; thus Schnee's and the son's activities were the focal point of our lines of vision. When the wheelbarrow was again filled with stones the son took the handles and pushed the barrow along the rut toward me. This time the wheel turned more easily since the mud was pressed firm in the groove, but this time the son had a harder time keeping the barrow balanced and I explained this to myself thus: when, the last time, the son was pushing the barrow through the more resistant mud, he had leaned more heavily over the handles and the middle axis of the barrow and had thus counteracted the tendency of the weight to tilt to the right or to the left, while now, when he was steering the total weight of the barrow just from the farthest ends of the handles, he had a heavier and more independent mass in front of him. I waved my hand, stretching it toward him and pulling it back, thus trying to suggest that he should lean farther toward the center of the barrow; and back at the house, Schnee, following the son with his eyes, made a gesture with his hand that started from his chest and went toward the son. But the son who only paid attention to keeping the wheel of the barrow in the rut made by the wheel didn't pay attention to my gesture and didn't turn to Schnee either which is how he could have noticed Schnee's motioning; he pushed the barrow toward me, only supporting it right and left

with his outstretched arms until he, right in front of the stacked wood, reached the spot where he, last time, had wanted to turn the barrow; and here the track had been hollowed out by the weight and the turning back and forth of the barrow; and the wheel got bogged in this hole; and the son's body was too far from the barrow to be able to keep the barrow, which was already tilting from too one-sided a pushing at the handles and from the increased pressure of stones rolling to that side, from tipping over; and so the barrow tipped over, at the same place as before.

I couldn't muster the energy to describe again how I climbed down from the stack of wood and helped the son pick up the stones; instead, after having written this last paragraph of my observations, after having gone to my room after picking up the stones, I lay down, lay down on my bed, put a few grains of salt in my eyes and saw, after a short blurred stage, a picture in front of me; or rather, I glided into the picture; I felt as if I were moving along a road, a wide asphalt road; I felt as if I were reclining comfortably in a car, a bus (I couldn't see the vehicle, it consisted only of a feeling of motion, of gliding), and while I was gliding along evenly and restfully, I saw, as far as the eye could reach, elk or deer lying along the road, huge animals, in pairs, copulating; the heads with the enormous antlers were raised high and from the gaping mouths rose the steam of hot breath. The hooves of each male animal hit the female shoulders and breast in a rough caress; and the rhythmic movements of the heavy bodies were accompanied by a hollow, giggly rattling from all the throats. While I glided along the unending row of animals the picture dissolved and the outlines of the room showed through. Looking at the outlines of the room through the still moving shadows of the animals, I heard, still listening for the sound of the bony clash of antlers, a knock at the door; and the knock washed away the last bits of the picture and made the room, with its walls, its objects, its window and its door come into focus, and after the knock, the door opened without my answering the knock; and the doctor entered the room, supporting himself on a cane, shut the door behind him and leaned against the wall fingering the bandaged and plastered spots on his head and face. His lips were moving, but I could not hear his voice; I sat up and put my hand to my ear, but there wasn't even a whisper; then I got up and went close to him and put my ear directly to his mouth, and now I could make out the following words from his breath and his tongue-motions: wounds not heal, whichever way I cut, hollow out deeply, down to the bone, knife on the bone, grates, scrapes, breaks off, sits deeper yet, bandage, all night, all night awake, still blood, pus, farther, down at the arm, then farther up, lifted, armpit, humerus, boil water, sprain, pain, bind, find, to the ribs, in the breast, deep in the breast, heart laid bare, lung, legs, plaster cast around the ankles, saws, clean cut, round the calves, shinbone cut,

tendons, plaster cast knee-high, thigh, deep in the ab-
domen, two pots of pus and blood, further in fury, and
now (here he took his black glasses off, and his eyes
were staring ahead with an empty, whitish shimmer)
nothing more to see, even the strongest light, all in the
dark, keep on, cutting in the dark, poise the knife, slide,
widen, grope, tap, overlap, instruments lost, lost, lost,
in the dark, swabs dropping, find ether, clamps, needle,
thread, wound open, at random, arm all slashed, lose
direction, lose the door, the table, wrong door, don't
know upstairs, downstairs, up or down, sit in the dark,
don't know arm or leg, pain the same, same pain, every-
where, wherever cut the same pain, drive out pain,
drown out, sing against; here he raised his voice and
started to bray half groaning and gnashing his teeth,
brayed, played, blade, brayed against the blade, by song
allayed, blood and voice be stayed. I supported his arm,
opened the door, led him out of my room, shut the door
behind us, led him through the garret to the stairs, and
on the way he kept braying: where, where does he lead
me, he the patient me the doctor, where, where does
he lead me, where, where does the patient lead the doctor; and when we had reached the stairs and I went
down backward before him, holding his arms and guid-
ing his stiff feet, he kept on braying: where, where, to
the stair, the stair, down the stair, down the down zigzag
stair, zigzag down the stair, down the downy stair, a wall
here and a wall there, we crawl along the wall, wall to
the hall, we crawl along the hall wall. Having reached

the hall I led him along the hall to the door of his room, and on this bit of the way he brayed: now on the plain, how bear the pain, life will remain, life will remain, who is with me, who is holding me, the patient, the patient the doctor; and when we had gotten to his door and I had pressed the handle down and led him into his room, he sang: open the door, open to the core, cut the sore, the pain gets more, and more and more, d'you hear the roar, who, who is with me, who in the room, what room, who, who; and when I had shut the door of his room behind us and led him to his bed and made him sit down, his braying faded into a monotonous *oooo* growing weaker and weaker and finally dying down. The four walls, the floor and the ceiling forming his room are furnished in such a way that, upon entering, one sees a long, coarse wooden table, so rough that it seems put together by the doctor's own hands, jutting out from right next to the door into the middle of the room where it touches a second table going to the right in a right angle which again touches a third table jutting out to the left in a right angle, nearly up to the window-wall opposite the door so that only a narrow space is left between the table and the wall; one can just squeeze through sideways, but with difficulty, and in doing so pass a window to the left, a small, high, round table full of tweezers, scalpels, needles, glasses, bottles, bowls and boxes that immediately joins a second such table, whereupon one is faced by three chairs stacked high with books, whereupon one turns to the right since the wall that forms right angles with the window-wall and the door-wall blocks the way; thus one leaves the just mentioned wall to the left and sees to the right, in the space between this wall and the rectangularly joined tables, a small, low, square table with a bowl of blood and, behind this table, a second, somewhat higher square table covered with bloody and pus-filled wads of cotton, whereupon one has reached the door-wall and can either turn back to the window-wall or climb under the first long table in order to get to the door again; in thought, I chose the latter, in order to examine the left half of the room, again starting from the door; there one finds first a high cabinet with glass doors, its shelves filled with innumerable brown, green and black labeled bottles as well as with boxes, packages, and bags labeled or at least written on, stamped, and numbered; whereupon one notices a leather armchair with some iodine-stained towels on the seat and the back, and then the iron bed painted white, after which just the bedside table at the head of the bed, also crammed with bottles, tubes, and boxes, has to be mentioned to complete the inventory of the doctor's room. In this room I stood now, after having set the doctor down on the bed, in front of the doctor's swaying body until the housekeeper, down in the hall, hit a spoon against the lid of a pot which was the signal for breakfast, whereupon two doors in the hall opened, the tailor's and the captain's, and I could hear, outside the house, the heavy, clomping steps of the hired man who must have moved with the horse from the field to the stable and from the stable to the kitchen door long before the housekeeper's signal, probably after having several times pulled out and snapped open his pocket watch, as well as the mother's voice calling the son from the window of the family's room, and Mr. Schnee's steps coming up from the yard toward the kitchen steps, and then my and the doctor's steps, since I had pulled the doctor up from the bed and led him again through the room to the door and from there, after having opened the door and closed it behind us, through the hall and down the stairs and through the hall to the kitchen where, with our arrival, all participants in the meal were gathered. Before we all sat down at the table, the housekeeper came up to the captain and lifted her pointed fingers to his back in order to remove a long, white thread sticking to his jacket in a wavy line. She picked the thread up, showed it to the captain who bent down and looked at it, and carried it to the sink where she let it drop; slowly it sank down. Now we sat down, took a slice each of the already cut bread, spread lard on it, and started eating it with the coffee the housekeeper poured from the blue pot into our mugs. Again the tailor's appetite was noticeable although the tailor had just left his bedroom, whereas the rest of us, except for the captain, had already spent a few hours moving around, partly in the house and partly outside; as for gobbling down his slice of bread, he nearly outdid the hired man who reeked with the smell of the plowed field. But when he tried to be the first to turn to a second slice, he suddenly stopped, froze in a gesture of surprise, reached into his mouth, and pulled out a tooth that must have loosened from his lower jaw during his violent chewing. He held the tooth in front of himself and stared at it. The captain said: a tooth. The housekeeper also said: a tooth. Mr. Schnee held his hand across the table under the tailor's hand holding the tooth and said: give me. The tailor lowered the tooth into Schnee's hand, Schnee took the tooth, wiped it with his handkerchief, looked at it and put it into the upper pocket of his jacket, saying: also teeth in my collection. The tailor put back the slice of bread he had already taken and sat immobile. The hired man ate on unconcerned. The doctor chewed his bread with difficulty. Mr. Schnee ate on. The housekeeper ate on. I ate on in order to stifle the suddenly rising feeling that this morning would never end.

Occasionally, when it is the birthday of one of the boarders, or on a holiday marked red in the calendar, or on any other day if she feels like it, the housekeeper invites us in the evening to a party in her room. It happened this evening. After supper, during which the housekeeper had invited us to visit her room, and after the family had been called too, everybody went to her room to drink his mug of coffee. Everyone went across the threshold holding the mug that had been filled with coffee in the kitchen, and went to the back of the room, passing first, to the right, an oval table with a lace tablecloth and a big purple glass vase, and, to the left, a chest of drawers with photographs of older and younger women, young girls, a child playing with a hoop, a baby on its belly, older and younger men, partly unbearded, partly with mustaches and beards, then walking along the back of a couch jutting out into the room on the one hand, and a square, also lace-covered table bearing a china statue, a shepherdess in crinoline with three sheep and a jumping dog, on the other, whereupon he went by, on the left, the tall column of a parchment-shaded lamp, and, on the right, by a low table, next to the couch, with round brass top on which there were a crystal bowl filled with colored balls of wool, a shell-covered box, a brass candleholder with a candle, not burning however, an inkpot, and an iron; in order to turn either to the right and be faced by two deeply cushioned armchairs, a high, black chair with corkscrew back posts, and another, silk-covered, oval table with a flesh-colored china dancer with bare breasts and legs and a loose gown, as well as a realistically colored wooden fawn and a cordial bottle and ten glasses on it, or to the left where he could see a wicker chair, a round table with a lamp with a silk shade, a leather armchair, a hassock, a footstool, a bedside table with marble top, a comb, scissors, a bowl of lard, a few hair curlers and a little potbellied bottle partly lying, partly standing on it, and the bed covered with a white woolen blanket. Aside from these chairs and tables among which we were now scattered, there were more

things and pieces of furniture along the walls; the foot
of the bed touched a washstand with a china water
bowl and water jug, a glass with a toothbrush, a soap-
holder, a hairbrush, a finger brush, and some hairpins;
above the washstand there was a mirror reflecting
some of the furniture and some of the guests; next to
the washstand stood a high wardrobe with closed
doors; above the bed was a picture showing a boar being chased by dogs and attacked by hunters armed with
spears in the thick of a forest, and a second picture at
the head of the bed, of a basket filled with violets. Once
the eye had gone along the window which was framed
by long heavy drapes of dark blue velvet and had a low
table full of potted plants in front of it, it came to a
treelike growth planted in a bucket, with large sword-
shaped leaves nearly reaching the ceiling, to another
round, lace-covered table with a lamp that had a shade
of glass beads and a music box, to another chest of
drawers filled with photographs also showing older
and younger men and women, here a house, there the
bay of a sea with a piece of beach and a few beach-
chairs among big round pebbles, here a high railway
bridge across a ravine, there a monument of a horse
and a horseman, here a lookout rising above trees, and
there a wide avenue of a city, to a half-open closet door,
to a carved black chair with high back over which a
picture showed snowy, moonlit hills, as well as, finally,
to another table, of wicker, bearing a big empty vase of
grainy clay painted with flowers. The housekeeper,

who had entered the room first, filled nine of the ten
glasses with the green cordial from the bottle, after
having put down her coffee cup on the table with the
bottle, and handed a glass to each of the guests who,
from all sides, each held out one arm toward her; because of the distance and hindering pieces of furniture
between, many of the guests could not reach the glass
in her hand, but had to take it from the hand of one of
the others, or from the hands of several of the other
guests standing between the remote guest and the
housekeeper; this caused a good deal of bowing forward and bowing to the side of the upper parts of the
bodies of those present, a circling, reaching out and
drawing back of arms, until everybody had gotten his
glass, and only one single empty glass was standing
beside the bottle. The housekeeper and the mother sat
down on the couch; opposite, in the deep armchairs,
the captain and Mr. Schnee were sitting, and, on the
high, black chair, the father, while the doctor sank
into the leather armchair, looking at the housekeeper's
and the mother's backs and at the back of the couch,
and the hired man chose the hassock, and the tailor the
footstool for a seat. I myself was standing at the window, the mug in one hand, the glass in the other; and
the son, who had not gotten a glass (it was the father
who had forbidden it; the housekeeper would certainly, as it happened once before, at just such a gathering as today's, have filled the last empty glass and
handed it to him, if the father's interference hadn't

kept her from doing so), was standing beside me, one
hand around his mug, the other cramped in the drapes,
in the drapes which he looked up at, tugging as if to
test how solid they were. Of the words the housekeeper, whose thighs were forced under the low table,
said to the mother who, hampered by the edge of the
oval table jutting over the back of the couch, was leaning diagonally toward the housekeeper, I understood
the following fragments: cook beans thoroughly, ham,
rind of bacon, melt fat, solid fat, lard, hole (whole);
whereupon I heard the mother say, while lifting her
glass and sipping at it: if sleeping, kicks off, blanket
slides, diapers wet, wakes me, milk gives out, always
sucking, today beans too (bean stew). Of the captain's
words addressed to Mr. Schnee, his legs crossed, sipping alternately at the mug and the glass, I caught: en-
joy leisure, right at rest, rare in former times, as at that
time; to which I heard Schnee answer, who had put his
mug on the table in front of him and was turning the
liqueur glass in his big, bony hands: work quite different (were quite different), something different, point
is, gathered together; whereupon the father turned to
him with the following audible words, pulling his chair
close to Schnee's armchair: relieved, in spite of all not
that easy, clumsy, sneaks, spokes, always stumbling
(tumbling), all the time stumbling, sure taken him to
task. Schnee answered: of course satisfied, I would,
strange, getting started is half, always hard battle, all a
matter of patience, without patience, together gathered collection together; his other words got lost in the

rising giggle of the housekeeper exclaiming: there you
could, some man; which the mother complemented
with the words: count to twenty, bridegrooms aplenty;
whereupon the housekeeper muttered something that
escaped me because at that moment the tailor turned
to the doctor with the following clear words: feel better, much better when weather better, in the back too,
always, get it in the back, before weather changes, rain
over, long enough, always the back, once two years ago,
no two, no two and a half years, so I couldn't get up, no
three years, get it in back, still farther back, last year
too, also the back, now better, sun all afternoon. The
doctor, the glass at his barely moving lips, spoke very
low: no improvement, not yet, expect any improvement, indifferent, what matter, what, yet, but gnawing;
drowned out by the words the hired man said to both
the doctor and the tailor: can confirm (cancan firm),
field the afternoon, wear me out, clouds, get clear, tell
by clouds, in the wrists and knees too, had an uncle,
drops he (dropsy, drop see), couldn't move; then again
a few laughing words from the housekeeper hit my ear:
so tasty, but tasty, had it at the station hotel, that time
at the station hotel, couldn't imagine better, or hardly;
the mother's laughing cut out the next words of which
I got only: shouldn't say, you know, understand; and
the mother added, with a side glance at the father: back
forth, back forth, drill, keep trying, fizzle, out; and
these words, in turn, got drowned in the housekeeper's
laughter. From the hired man I then heard: still had the

cow, leading the bull, cart coming, was the coachman, still coming, lift block, bull out, smelled already, foam at the mouth, crash with the horns, held the cow, didn't want, tied up, tail, ram in; at which the doctor leaned over to the hired man and asked: was cow long ago, never seen, before my time; to which the hired man answered: miscarriage, slaughtered, loss, not worth it, farming, without help, strength, wrack and ruin; here the doctor said, opening the safety pin of his head bandage: several years ago, or months; and then, calling over to the housekeeper: how long actually here, when did come. The housekeeper wasn't listening; she said to the mother: take up (take cup), sew up, hem up, put on collar (color), show skirt, wear hat, go to town, often intend, never get around; whereupon the mother pointed at the closet and said: ostrich feather, wonderful white, be smart, dancing, with music; whereupon the housekeeper called over to the son: wind the box, music box, wind, key inside, hear music. The son hunched over the music box and turned the key to wind the creaky works. I heard the spring beginning to crack inside the box, and I was already lifting my hand to warn him that he mustn't turn any more if he didn't want to break the spring, but it was too late; hardly had I lifted my hand than there was a snapping sound, followed by a short clattering and rattling; the son was standing motionless, his hand on the key. The housekeeper jumped up knocking over a half-full coffee mug; the coffee ran over the table and into the lap of the mother who couldn't move away fast enough; the housekeeper heaved herself sideways past the father, Schnee and the captain and hit the glass the captain was holding in front of himself; and the contents of the glass, only a few drops, it is true, ran down the lapel of his cutaway; the mother, shaking her skirt and squeezing by the table, caught her foot on the leg of the table, losing her shoe; then she stumbled toward the father who had time enough to open his arms to catch her, but not time to put down the mug in one hand and the glass in the other, which made both coffee and liqueur splatter over both the mother's dress and the father's pants. The housekeeper, her hands ready to grab the key to the music box (which was to come loose in her hand), in sweeping by caught the iron on the table with the bow of her apron strings; and the iron fell on something which had been withdrawn the moment the housekeeper ran by, but which immediately pushed forward again: Mr. Schnee's foot; and the iron striking drew a loud scream from him, whereupon he bent all the way down over his hurt foot and blew, with a whistling sound, on the shoe. The housekeeper had now reached the key, with her hands far ahead of her and her legs still a jump behind; the son had let go of the key and retreated; the key turned, as I had expected, loosely in the box without resistance. Box kaputt, the housekeeper cried: take to town, repair. The father screamed: right now, tonight, take, get to town tomorrow morning, right away to the locksmith, right away, get the lead out, all night. I took the music box and the key which had slipped out into the housekeeper's hand and handed the music box and the key to the son; the son, his head on his chest, looked at me from below, with the bluish white of his eyeballs shining around the black iris, then he went hastily, the box under his arm and the key in his hand, through the room, past the back of the couch, the tables and the chest of drawers, opened the door, stepped out, closed the door behind him, and went away through the hall and down the stairs. We could still hear the kitchen door snapping shut. In the room, the talking started up again after the silence which accompanied the son's departure. There was talk about the broken music box, about the iron, about Mr. Schnee's foot, about the spilled coffee and liqueur, about the spots in the clothes, and after a while, the lines of thought began to branch out more and more from the events which had just happened: from the words of the housekeeper and the mother, who had both returned to the couch, the housekeeper from the table where the music box had been, and the mother from the father's lap where she had sat down, one could conclude that they were talking about aprons, blouses, skirts, bonnets, ribbons, and hats; and from the words of Mr. Schnee who was again leaning back in his armchair, and the words of the captain, who had wiped the stain on his vest with his handkerchief, I could make out that they were speaking of pressed pants, shoe models, polished and unpolished shoes, riding boots, horses, and a wine cellar in the garrison town; and from the remarks which the father made, whose face had turned a bluish red during the accident with the music box and returned to its natural color after the son had disappeared, I could understand that they were about corporal punishment, running the gauntlet, hanging, decapitating, imprisonment, drowning, burning, and banishment. The circle of conversations ran on and on and blended into a general though diversified buzzing, while the doctor, who had hardly paid attention to the incident of the music box, but had gone on unrolling his head bandage with one hand and rolling it into a ball with the other, loosened the last bloody, sticky piece of bandage from his forehead, and while the hired man, with a throaty cooing, pulled the cards from his pocket, shuffled the cards, and divided them between himself and the tailor who had moved his footstool closer to the hired man. The hired man threw a few cards on the floor in front of him and said: a jack and a nine; and the tailor threw a card beside the cards on the floor and said: a three; and the hired man right away threw two new cards beside the cards on the floor and exclaimed: a king and a two; whereupon the tailor threw two of his cards next to the cards on the floor crying: king and ace. The exhausted doctor was leaning his head against the back of the armchair; on his forehead, a large, festering wound was showing which he touched lightly and cautiously with the little finger of his left hand. The housekeeper and the mother got up, talking about dress hems, mother-of-pearl buttons, corset hooks, hat pins and brooches, and, smoothing their dresses with their hands, went sideways past the oval table, past the father's chair, past the wicker table with the clay lamp, and past the other empty, black chair to the closet door, slid the closet door open completely, and went into the clothes-filled space, the housekeeper first, the mother pulling the door shut behind them as she crossed the threshold. Hardly had the door clicked shut than we heard muted shouting from within among which the following words were recognizable: lock, get open, push, pull, locked in, whereupon there were knocks against the inside of the door. All but the doctor turned toward the closet door, remaining, however, seated a few moments longer while the knocking grew stronger, then, having caught on to what had happened, they jumped up, the father first, the captain second, Schnee third, the hired man fourth, the tailor last (I stayed at the window), and ran as fast as they could between the chairs, tables, lamps, chests, and plants to the closet door. Where is the key, the father shouted at the door which the captain's fist hit at the same moment; the key, where is it, he shouted once more, but with the captain's knocking one couldn't hear the answer from within. The father got hold of the captain's hand and shouted once again: where key; and from within the hollow answer: is no key. Is no key, the captain asked back from the outside, and while incomprehensible words were shouted from the inside, the father repeated: no key. Where the key, the hired man called, and Schnee said to the hired man is no key, key gone, while the housekeeper's voice behind the door shouted something incomprehensible. Is key gone, the father called to the door, and from the inside we could hear indistinctly: key gone, break open, suffocating, and the father shouted: break door open or will suffocate, and already was throwing his weight forcefully against the door which, however, did not give in to his barrage. Then the captain threw himself against the door which resisted him as well, and it also resisted the hired man and Mr. Schnee who rushed against the door together. Get an ax, said the father, and the hired man called to the door, get the ax, wait, just to the shed, get the ax, then he turned around, ran past the wicker table with the vase and the oval table with the vase, climbed over the couch and ran to the door, opened the door, left it open behind him, ran through the hall, downstairs, through the downstairs hall, through the kitchen, threw open the kitchen door, ran out, leaving the kitchen door open behind him, down the steps and across the yard to the shed; I saw him crossing the streak of light that was falling on the ground from the window. In the closet, the mother and the housekeeper were screaming and hitting the door; and outside, the father, the captain, Mr. Schnee, and the tailor were screaming at the door: back right away, calm down, just the ax, be back right away, cut door open, right away, open right away. Then the hired man came from the shed, came running from the dark into the streak of light from the window, flew up the steps to the kitchen door, over the threshold of the kitchen door, pulled the kitchen door shut behind him, ran through the kitchen, the hall, up the stairs, along the hall, and into the room, slamming the door behind him. He jumped across the couch one hand supported on the back, the other waving the ax. The father reached for the ax, and the hired man shoved the ax toward him, then the father lifted the ax, while all the others drew back from the door, and called: I'm going to chop now, and drove the ax into the lock of the door. The ax went deep into the wood. The hired man helped the father, who was laboriously tugging at the handle, to pull the ax out of the wood; then the father drove the ax again into the door, tugged again, with the hired man helping, at the ax which had sunk deep into the wood; but this time the ax did not come out, but broke off at the head of the shaft. In the closet, the house-keeper and the mother, who had calmed down during the work, were again pounding against the door and shouting words of which I caught: hot and air (scared). Mr. Schnee lifted his hand and cried: go for the crow-bar, and ran between the chairs and tables, past the couch and the chest of drawers, to the door, opened the door, leapt over the threshold leaving the door open behind him, disappeared through the hall, the stairs, the downstairs hall, the kitchen, the kitchen door which he left open behind him, and the kitchen steps, popped up in the streak of light below the window, and disappeared again in the dark. Just go to the bar, the father shouted at the door, and the captain shouted: gone for the crowbar; just gone for the crowbar, the father shouted, right back, break the door open, ax broken, break the door with the bar with crowbar; and the housekeeper cried inside, behind the door: heat, stifling. Schnee with the crowbar appeared in the light, ran through the brightness, up the kitchen stairs, through the kitchen door which he left open behind him, through the kitchen, the hall, up the stairs, along the hall, and appeared, the crowbar raised high in his hand, on the threshold which he leapt across, slamming the door behind him, racing past the furniture in a curve through the room to the closet door. The hired man took the crowbar from him and thrust it, together with the father, between the jamb and the door; and they shoved and tugged at the crowbar until the wood of the door started to crack and splinter. After they had rammed the crowbar several times into the splitting wood around the lock and pulled it out again with combined strength, and driven it in between the door and the jamb, the door began to loosen; the wood bent, apparently under the weight of the bodies of the housekeeper and the mother pressing from inside, and finally the door split open, didn't give way to one side, however, but, having slid off the hinges, fell forward, on the father's head. He staggered backward, and at the same time the housekeeper and the mother staggered out of the closet, over the door into the room. In

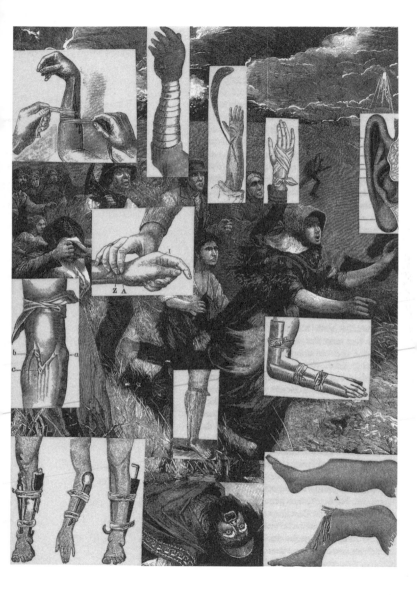

the hurly-burly of simultaneous movements, the hired man bent over the door, and Schnee over the crowbar, the father rubbed his head, the housekeeper and the mother stumbled to the couch, the hired man lifted the door and Schnee the crowbar, the housekeeper and the mother sat down on the couch, the tailor picked up wood splinters from the floor, the father put a pillow on his head, the hired man leaned the door against the closet jamb, Schnee put the crowbar in the corner to the right of the closet, the captain filled his glass, the housekeeper lifted the captain's coffee mug and the mother the housekeeper's coffee mug, the father tottered past the chairs with the pillow on his head, the captain emptied his glass, the housekeeper and the mother slurped what was left in the mugs, the doctor, who even during the incident with the closet door had been sitting unconcerned in his armchair, his head leaning back, got up, the father moved past the big, sword-leaved plant and me, the tailor picked up the splinters he had gathered into a heap, the doctor went through the room with the rolled-up bandage in one hand, leaning on the backs of the chairs, the couch, and the chest of drawers with the other, the father opened the window and, catching hold of the drapes with one hand, leaned out of the window, the housekeeper and the mother leaned back on the couch, Schnee sat down in his armchair, the doctor opened the door, the hired man went to the cards spread out on the floor, the tailor went between the pieces of furniture through the room with the wood splinters under his arm, the doctor left the room, pulling the door shut behind him, the father straightened up, pulling at the drapes, the captain balanced on his toes, his hands on his back under his tails, the drapes, probably loosened already by the son's tugging, together with the curtain rod and the wood around it, fell down hitting the father's head and knocking down the potted plants, the father scrambled out from under the cloth of the drapes, the housekeeper, followed by the mother, jumped up from the couch, the tailor dropped his wood at the door, the hired man looked up from the cards and at the window, the captain ran past Schnee to the father, kicking chairs and stools aside, Mr. Schnee got out of his armchair, the mother, squeezing by between Schnee and the table, took the father's arm, the hired man walked over to the knocked-down pots, I stretched my arm into the cold draft from outside and shut the window, the mother put her arm around the father and led him through the furniture to the door, the tailor bent over the fallen wood, Schnee sank back into his chair, the hired man picked up the pots with a throaty hum, the captain and I picked up the wood molding with the curtain rod and the drapes on it, the housekeeper and the hired man put the pots back on the plant table, the mother opened the door, the tailor picked up the wood, the mother and the father crossed the threshold, the captain and I rolled up the drapes, the housekeeper went sideways by the armchairs, grazing Schnee's head, and by the chest with the photographs to the closet, the captain and I put the drapes with the rod and the wood around it in the corner next to the chest of drawers, the housekeeper brought a broom from the closet, the mother shut the door behind herself and the father, the captain returned to his armchair, the tailor straightened up with the picked-up wood, Mr. Schnee filled his glass, the tailor opened the door, the housekeeper with the broom came to the window, the captain poured himself more liqueur from the bottle, the tailor crossed the threshold, the housekeeper swept the earth spilled from the pots, the tailor shut the door behind him, the hired man went back to the cards, the captain lifted the glass to his mouth, I went by the tables, the chairs, the back of the couch, the chest of drawers, to the door, the hired man picked the cards up from the floor, I opened the door, the wood of the housekeeper's broom hit the wall and the legs of the plant table, I crossed the threshold and shut the door behind me.

The day following this night I spent, until dusk, describing the evening which I have just finished describing. Sitting at the table in my room I look through the garret window and see beyond the edge of the sloping roof a piece of the muddy yard limited by the wood stack, the woodshed, the heap of stones, and the grange. In the moist purple furrows, the hired man is clomping behind the plow pulled by the horse; and over the broken earth a crow is flapping which, because of its single cry (which, as I now remember, I had heard earlier today while writing) I suspect to be the same crow I had heard crying harm over the fields two days ago when I started writing. The sky above the woods beyond the fields back of the plowing hired man is a burning, bloody red; the shadow of the hired man, the plow, and the horse is lying long and wavy on the furrows beneath the fluttering shadow of the crow; the shadow of the house goes up to the wood stack, the shed, and the heap of stones; beside it, long and narrow, the shadow of the outhouse, and the shadow of the grange is spread hugely over the fields, topped by the shadow of a human figure. The man throwing the shadow on the roof of the grange is the father who, his legs clamped around the ridge, is watching the dirt road with binoculars in spite of the repeated call echoing against the wall of the grange and coming most likely from the mother leaning out of the window of the family's room: much much too early early, won't be back back for a long a long time. I can tell the passage of time by the sky changing from burning red to rust brown, and by the shadows creeping farther out into the fields and blurring their outlines. Then, within a few seconds (the sun sinks behind the horizon opposite) the shadows spill inkily over the ground; the hired man is up to his knees in darkness, only his face is still glowing red; and the darkness climbs up the wall of the grange whose roof is still reflecting the last of the sunlight; then the hired man's face is extinguished, and then the roof of the grange; the father's face and the shiny metal knob of the binoculars stay longest in the sun, until even the colors of the father's face and the binoculars grow dull, and everything is covered in a single gloomy shadow, the shadow of the earth. Now the father raises his arm and, pointing toward the dirt road, turns to the house and shouts, probably to the mother he no doubt sees in the window: it's coming, the coach, the coach is coming. I raise the window and lean out and see, far back on the dirt road, something dark approaching slowly and gradually taking the shape of a coach with a horse.

As always at the approach of the coach, announced from afar by the coachman's horn signal, the boarders, except for the doctor who stayed at the threshold of the kitchen door, went out in front of the house and gathered by the side of the road in order to wait there for the coach, together with the housekeeper and the hired man who both had left their work, whatever it was, as they always did for the arrival of the coach, and had gone to the middle of the road. In the growing darkness, the horse moved toward us, not galloping and not running, but in a slow trot, and behind it the reeling coach with the coachman's outline high on the box; and the speed or slowness of the approach was in exact proportion to the increasing darkness, so that the coach would have been swallowed by the dark had it stood still, but since it moved, it constantly balanced the degree of increased darkness by the degree of approaching speed, but it also stayed blurred because of the increasing darkness, so that, when it finally stood right in front of us, it had gained only in size, but was still just as foglike and smoldering, just as embedded in the deep dusk as before. The previous moment of the coachman's tightening the reins and telling the horse to stop with the drumming sound of his tongue was three days and three nights ago, three days and three nights in which I couldn't bring myself to continue my notes because of an absolute indifference; and even now I can only continue with difficulty the description of the coach's arrival and what followed, ready to break off at any moment and to give it up for good. After the stopping of the horse, three days and three nights ago, the coachman got down from the box, greeting the housekeeper by shaking hands with her, greeting the hired man by waving his hand at him, and greeting the rest of us by nodding at us, except for the doctor, back at the front door whom he didn't notice. He was dressed in a wide leather coat, and wore a broad-rimmed felt hat with a few dappled partridge feathers stuck in the band. His legs, in polished boots of brown leather, walked as if they had springs in the hollow of the knee. His horn was hanging on a strap over his shoulder. The father and the mother opened the door of the coach, leaned far into it, turned away and walked back to the house, shaking their heads. The hired man too looked into the coach; he thrust in his arms and pulled out a sack, filled with coal to judge by the external shape; it could also have been filled with potatoes, but this possibility was ruled out since the house had its own potato field and, for that reason, didn't need to order potatoes from the town. Bending his knees, the hired man pressed his back against the sack, raised his hands over his shoulders, lowered them behind his shoulders, grabbed the sack, straightened his legs, bent forward holding the sack on his back, and went toward the kitchen steps, past the kitchen steps and toward the basement steps, down the basement steps to the basement door which he kicked open. The coachman also reached into the coach and pulled out a sack, bent his knees, pulled the sack onto his back with his arms raised high, straightened his leather-rustling legs, and carried, bent forward, the sack to the basement, after the hired man. The hired man had turned on the light in the basement, and broad and black, the coachman entered the light shaft of the basement stairs. The sound of the sack being emptied down in the basement confirmed my conjecture that the sack contained coal. The emptying of the coachman's sack made the same sound; besides, I followed the coachman and thus could verify with my own eyes that it was coal which fell dustily from the sacks in the wooden partition next to the furnace. The hired man turned to the basement door, folding the empty sack, went to the basement door and through the door, up the stairs, across the yard, past the kitchen steps; and the coachman followed the hired

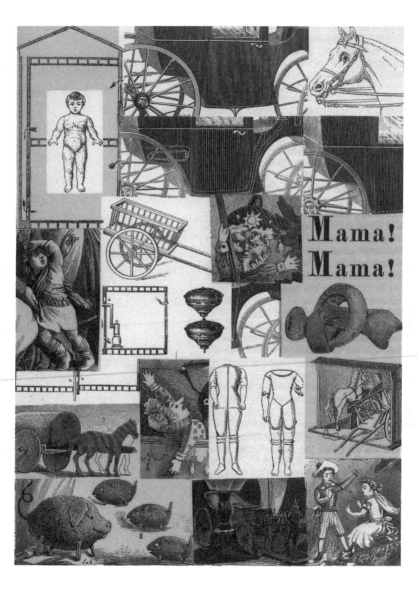

Mama!
Mama!

man, also folding his sack; outside there were voices and steps which suggested that the housekeeper and the boarders were going back into the house. The hired man showed up again with a full sack on his back, a sack he emptied over the partition and carried back empty and folded, meeting the coachman who was also carrying a new sack on his back, a new full sack which he, like the hired man, emptied, folded and carried back, meeting the hired man, who again carried a full sack on his back, a full sack that was emptied, folded, and taken back, when the coachman showed up again, a sack on his back whose contents he poured onto the coal heap over the partition, a sack which was folded and taken away just like the sack of the hired man who now showed up with it again, and like the next sack of the coachman's and the next sack of the hired man's and all the following sacks of which I lost count. What I didn't understand, considering the large number of sacks and the size of the coal heap, was how all these sacks filled with coal had found room in the coach which hadn't even seemed fully loaded; and after I had gone back and forth several times between the coach and the coal heap in order to compare the spaces, this became even more incomprehensible. Had there been sacks on the top of the roof; the coachman whom I asked denied it; and what reason could he have to lie to me; also I would certainly have noticed them at the arrival, and, with a load of sacks behind him, the coachman's outline wouldn't have stood out as clearly above the coach as it had while the coach was coming nearer. During the meal, which the coachman ate on the free place to my left, I asked him again: don't you think, coachman, that the heap of coal in the basement is by far greater than the capacity of the coach, and how do you explain that; to which he answered without looking up from his spoon full of potatoes and beans: just illusion. Unsatisfied by his answer I turned to the hired man and asked him: didn't it strike you too, hired man, that the amount of coal in the basement is larger than could have found room in the coach; which he answered this way, chewing potatoes and beans in his mouth: in sacks tighter, heap more loosely, no wonder. But this explanation didn't satisfy me either, even though both the coachman's and the hired man's words may have contained a grain of truth; and even today, three days and three nights later, I haven't found an explanation for the unproportionately large difference between the space the coal could fill in the coach and the space it filled in the basement. Fighting hard against my sleepiness and my impulse to put the pencil down and give up these notes, I think back to the evening three days and three nights ago and go on describing this thinking back; and the fourth night is already beginning with supper finished and me having withdrawn from the boarders gathered in the hall; the fourth night after the evening when the coachman, after we had left the gathering in the hall for our rooms, followed the housekeeper who was carrying the coffee mugs into the kitchen to the sink, followed her into the kitchen and stayed there with her, which I could see from the shadows falling from the kitchen window onto the ground in the yard while I was leaning out of my window inhaling the night air. As I calculated, the shadows must be thrown by the bulb of the adjustable lamp in the middle of the kitchen, and considering the position of the shadows, the lamp must have been pulled down to chest height, probably to light up the floor which the housekeeper intended to scrub; I therefore distinctly saw the shadow of the coffeepot stick up over the shadow of the windowsill, and, to the side, about from the place where the house-keeper sat at meals, the shadow of the housekeeper bent over the table with arms stretched out and the shadow of the coffeepot. Now the coachman's shadow, rising from the back of the kitchen and growing beyond the shadow of the edge of the table on the same level as the shadow of the windowsill, appeared next to the housekeeper's shadow; the shadow of his arms reached into the shadow of the housekeeper's arm, and also the housekeeper's other arm joined the now swelling shadow of the arms, whereupon the shadow mass of the housekeeper's body came close to the shadow mass of the coachman's body and fused with it. Only the shadow of the housekeeper's raised hand holding the coffeepot stuck out from the shapeless, condensed joining of the bodies' shadows. The shadow of the coffeepot swayed back and forth, the shadow of the bodies also swayed back and forth; and now and then the shadow of the heads in profile, sticking close to-gether, rose above the clump of the bodies. After a violent side movement of the bodies, the shadow of the coffeepot broke free from the shadow of the hand and fell down; for a few seconds, the shadows of the bodies came apart; the housekeeper's body with the arching breast line leaned back on the table; the coachman's shadow opened and rose up high with wild gestures and as if flapping his wings, throwing off the bulk of his coat's shadow. After the coat shadow had slid off the shadow of the coachman's body, the shadow of the coachman's body thrust forward again, and the shadow of the housekeeper's body came to meet him with the shadows of the housekeeper's arms reaching into the shadow of the coachman's body, beyond and around it, and the shadows of the coachman's arms dug into the shadow of the housekeeper's body and around it. With jerky, jolting movements, the shadows of the bodies turned and edged farther toward the middle of the shadow of the windowsill and table edge; the shadows of the housekeeper's legs (she was lying on the table) rose with bent knees above the shadow of the coach-man's body as it crept forward; and the shadow of the coachman on his knees rose above the shadow of the housekeeper's belly. The shadow of the coachman's hands delved into the shadow of the housekeeper's skirt; the shadow of the skirt slid back; and the shadow of the coachman's belly burrowed into the shadow of the housekeeper's bared thighs. The shadow of one of the coachman's arms bent toward the shadow of his lower body and pulled out a rodlike shadow which, in form and position, corresponded to his sexual organ; this questing shadow he thrust in the heavy, full shadow of the housekeeper's body, after the shadows of the housekeeper's legs had risen to the shadow of the coachman's shoulders. The shadow of the coachman's lower body rose and sank in an accelerating rhythm over the responsive, dancing shadow of the housekeeper's body while the shadows of their heads remained locked in profile. Finally, the shadow of the housekeeper's body reared up, and the shadow of the coachman's body threw itself with full force into the shadow of the housekeeper's body, whereupon the shadows of both bodies, fusing, broke down and stayed stretched out on the shadow of the table, rising and falling in heavy respiration. After a while, the coachman's shadow rose and moved away from the housekeeper's shadow, and the housekeeper's shadow also rose up; and from further movements of the shadows I gathered that both the coachman and the housekeeper left the table and went to the back of the kitchen where their doings were hidden from me. Shortly after they had gotten up from the table I heard the kitchen door open; then I saw the housekeeper and the coachman go down the kitchen steps and across the yard to the coach. I could not make out the coach in the dark; I could only conclude from the sounds that the coachman was getting the coach and the horse ready for the return trip; and sure enough, soon afterward, the shaft, the bridle, and the wheels began creaking, and the horse's steps clattered on the road, resounding further and further away, as did the rattling and squeaking and creaking of the coach, until it died down altogether in the silence of the night. And this too, the fact that the horse, after having pulled the load of coal for such a long way during most of the day, had to go back the same way the night following this same day, this made me wonder, so that I couldn't get to sleep that night, three days and almost four nights ago

# Afterword

Peter Weiss was not a young man when *The Shadow of the Coachman's Body,* his first book in German, appeared in 1960. He had already been a painter, an experimental filmmaker, and an author of both fiction and short plays in Swedish. The book not only marked his transition from writing in Swedish to writing in German, but also from the visual arts to a focus on writing, at least to a degree: *The Shadow of the Coachman's Body* includes seven collages by Weiss that, picking up its motifs, visually extend the mosaic of the writing.

*The Shadow of the Coachman's Body* was immediately acclaimed by German critics for its remarkable use of and focus on language. It was followed by two autobiographical books, *Abschied von den Eltern (Leavetaking),* and *Fluchtpunkt (Vanishing Point),* which added to his renown. But it took his 1964 play, *The Persecution and Assassination of Jean-Paul Marat as Performed by the Inmates of the Asylum of Charenton Under the Direction of the Marquis de Sade,* commonly known as *Marat/Sade,* to bring Weiss international fame.

Born in Berlin in 1916, the son of a Czech-Jewish

textile manufacturer and a Swiss mother, Weiss was raised as a Protestant. As an adolescent, he thought only about writing, painting, and music, but also felt "blindly drawn along" by the Nazi marches and speeches.

> Had I not suddenly been faced with a drastic change I would have been borne along in the torrent of marching columns, into my destruction. This sudden change took place after hearing one of the speeches which in those days spewed out of the loudspeakers and which before my realization possessed an inconceivable power over me.... Next to me sat Gottfried, my half brother.... And when the hurricane of jubilant summons to death and self-sacrifice ... had run its course, Gottfried said, What a pity you can't be with us.... And when Gottfried then explained that my father was a Jew, this came to me like the confirmation of something I had long suspected. *

Weiss now understood why he had been bullied so much by the neighborhood boys. He became fully conscious of being an outsider. This was the fundamental experience of his life and a condition he continued to feel deeply when he was a refugee in Sweden.

As he writes in his essay "Meine Ortschaft" (My place), the many cities he had lived in became a blur, mere points of transit, whereas "the place for which I was destined but which I managed to escape" was Auschwitz, which "I have seen only twenty years later." **

* *Exile* (Delacorte Press, 1968), pp. 43–44. This volume contains both *Leavetaking* and *Vanishing Point*.

** *Rapporte* (Suhrkamp, 1968), p. 114.

However, after years of searching for his way through Swedish books, paintings, and films, he, like Paul Celan, was able at last to find a "place" in the language of his childhood while separating it from Germany:

> The language that now asserted itself ... the natural language that was my tool and now belonged to me alone and had nothing more to do with the land where I had grown up. This language was present whenever I wanted it and wherever I was.... And if it was hard to find the right words and images this was not because I did not belong anywhere ... but only because many words and pictures lay so deep down that they had to be long sought for. *

The moment that he realized this he realized that it was possible for him to live and work in this world: he could write in German, participate in the exchange of ideas around him, and not be bound to any country.

Weiss has said that it was his condition as an outsider that made him an ardent observer of everything around him (though in *Leavetaking* he remembers that already as a child he was always *looking*: at rooms, streets, courtyards, the play of light and shadow, the movement of eyes and hands). The narrator of *The Shadow of the Coachman's Body* incarnates this state of being. He is almost totally reduced to being an observer and writer. There are only two moments when, trying to help an oppressed son, he goes into rather futile action.

* *Exile*, pp. 244f

In the first of the ten sections of the novella the narrator is sitting in the outhouse of what seems to be a rural boarding house. He records very systematically and in precise detail what he hears and what the half-open door allows him to see. The description includes his own position of sitting in the outhouse. He also notes that the coachman has not arrived yet and therefore could not be the one handling the saw he hears. Throughout the novella we are made aware of an absence. At every meal, in every round of description of hands, mouths, there is obsessive mention of the empty place on the narrator's left, the spot that will eventually be filled by the coachman.

The structure of this first section is a small-scale mirror of the entire narrative, which oscillates between observation of what is outside and description of the narrator's own physical position as well as of his doubts, his attempts at turning his observations into writing, and his adding "inner images" by putting salt in his eyes. It also contains a first pointer to his method of writing: the toilet paper is cut-up newspapers, so that the would-be reader gets mixed up fragments of information. Just so the narrator will throughout jump from one physical detail to another, from one person's speech to mishearing another's.

The longest sections are naturally given to the narrator's outside observations. He turns his sharp eye on the evening meal that unites all the boarders. Beginning with the seating order of all the guests, he describes in turn every hand raising a plate toward the housekeeper, everybody's way of holding the spoon, the look of the mouths, their manner of chewing, the way their fingers grasp their mugs. Weiss's mosaic of serial bodily details transforms a mundane occurrence into a grotesque spectacle. It is closer to the spatial simultaneity of painting or collage than to any traditional "narrative thread."

This will become even clearer later, when an evening party in the housekeeper's room turns into pandemonium—a music box is broken, two people are locked in a closet, drapes get pulled down from the window, and the simultaneous movements of all the boarders tumble through one long sentence in Chaplinesque slapstick.

The last section brings the long-anticipated arrival of the coachman. This, the narrator tells us, happened three days and three nights before his writing about it, a time during which he was unable to sleep or write. Even now it's only with the greatest difficulty that he is able to continue. He had observed how, after dinner, the shadow of the coachman's body was projected outside the kitchen window in the act of having sex with the shadow of the housekeeper's body on the shadow of the kitchen table. This shadow play severely upset our writer. It made him aware of what was lacking in his life. It also cast doubt on his efforts to write. No matter how much his perspective has widened from the half-open door of the outhouse to his wide-open attic window, no matter how precisely he has tried to focus on life's basic processes (the novella begins with excretion, is occupied with eating throughout, and ends with sex)—what he is able to translate onto paper is never life, but at best a shadow.

The novella leaves us with the narrator in torment. The relation of art and life, the problem of the writer's place in the world, especially a world that calls for political engagement, will continue to be Weiss's theme throughout all his following works.

ROSMARIE WALDROP